For my mom, for leading by example,
enjoying and appreciating the
most beautiful parts of parenthood.

A FEIWEL AND FRIENDS BOOK

An Imprint of Macmillan

BATHTIME WITH THEO AND BEAU. Copyright © 2016 by Jessica Shyba. All rights reserved.
Printed in China by RR Donnelley Asia Printing Solutions Ltd., Dongguan City, Guangdong Province.
For information, address Feiwel and Friends, 175 Fifth Avenue, New York, N.Y. 10010.

Feiwel and Friends books may be purchased for business or promotional use. For information
on bulk purchases, please contact the Macmillan Corporate and Premium Sales Department
at (800) 221-7945 x5442 or by e-mail at specialmarkets@macmillan.com.

Library of Congress Cataloging-in-Publication Data Available

ISBN: 978-1-250-05907-9

Book design by April Ward

Feiwel and Friends logo designed by Filomena Tuosto

First Edition: 2016

1   3   5   7   9   10   8   6   4   2

mackids.com

Bathtime with
Theo & Beau

Jessica Shyba

Feiwel and Friends
NEW YORK

Beau is **dirty**.

Theo is **dirty.**

It must be
bathtime!

First
we
get in.

UP
you go.

Time to get
clean.

Add some water....

and
bubbles
for
fun.

Is it
time to
play?

Rubber duckies
save the day!

Find the

soap...

and scrub,
scrub, scrub.

Rinse with
water
and
shake
it off.

Are we
done?

Over and **out** we go.

Grab a
towel

or maybe
two.

We're all clean
and dry ...

until our next
bathtime!

Love you,
Theo.

Love you,
Beau.

Adoption Story

Our dream to get a puppy officially kicked into gear Christmas 2012. We had trekked our three excited kids—Jack (age 5), Zoe (age 4), and Beau (age 1)—twelve blocks to Macy's in Herald Square on a blustery day to meet the wish-granter himself. Jack and Zoe perched themselves on Santa's lap and asked, in unison, for a puppy. My husband Justin and I gasped in disbelief!

With a pending move to California and dogs being forbidden in our building in NYC, we were facing a conversation that we had hoped to avoid for at least another year. It was a hard moment for us as parents. We wanted to instill in the kids the idea that having a puppy was a big responsibility—one to be earned—and that a puppy would need attention and love.

When we moved to California in August 2013, we began looking at local animal shelters for a dog to adopt. The children came with us on more than one occasion, and each time we left without a puppy, my heart broke.

Justin and I couldn't agree on what kind of dog would be best for our family. One was too tiny, the next too hairy, the next too jumpy.

Then, on our fourth visit, we found our puppy tucked together with his two siblings in the backyard of the Santa Cruz SPCA. He was the shyest of them all, but bounded instantly into Beau's lap as soon as Beau entered the pen. The look on the puppy's face quickly convinced us that we had met our newest family member. We decided to name him Theo, partly because it was my grandfather's name, and partly because it just sounded right.

Theo is very much an old soul with a heart full of love for everyone in our family—including the newest member, Evangeline—but his bond with Beau remains something special. They do everything together from playtime to naptime to bathtime.

I'm not sure how we got so lucky to bring this particularly perfect pup into our lives, but he has changed all of us for the better. There's a reason they call Rescue Dogs their very own breed. They are unique and loving, and I'm so glad Theo chose us.

Jessica Shyba